The Good King

Ronald Wayne Fry

Illustrated by
Terry Werntz

Copyright © 2013 by Ron Fry. 137153-WERN
Library of Congress Control Number: 2013914756

ISBN: Softcover   978-1-4836-8500-7
        Hardcover   978-1-4836-8501-4
        EBook   978-1-4836-8502-1

This is a work of fiction. Names, characters, places
and incidents either are the product of the author's
imagination or are used fictitiously, and any resemblance
to any actual persons, living or dead, events, or locales is
entirely coincidental.

Rev. date: 08/23/2013

To order additional copies of this book, contact:
Xlibris LLC
1-888-795-4274
www.Xlibris.com

To CALEB,
ENJOY Following
Patch AND FRIENDS
AS they Look FoR
"THE Good King"
Terry Werntz

Long, long, long ago
When pirates sailed the seas
There was a rascal
His name was Patch
"That's CAP'N Patch, if you please!"

Now ol' Cap'n Patch was
a typical pirate
He would drink and steal and swear
"But now it's time to be
nice and find a home
"Where folks are kind and fair!"

"My Mum was right," the Cap'n said
"A pirate's life is bad!
"It's not nice to be a crook
"And steal what others have!"

"If only I could find a place
"A country I could stay.
"But what kind of king
would let a pirate in?
"THAT would be the day!"

Just then Patch heard a wiggle
Coming from the chest!
He opened the box
And there they were!
"Oh boy! Now HERE'S a mess!"

In the chest were stowaways!
In fact, they were two kids!
"Howdy, Cap'n! We're Flip and Flop!
"Thanks for flipping our lid!"

"We have no Moms
"We have no Dads.
"We thought we'd take a trip!
"We hitched a ride and came to town
"And then we found your ship!"

"We're out to sea! We can't go back!"
Patch shaded his eyes and looked
"But if I'm caught with you two squids
"My goose is REALLY cooked!"

Then Patch had an idea!
"I know what we will do!
"I'm very sure that this will work
"I've thought it through and through!"

"We all need a home, we do
"Let's stick together, us three!
"You squids both need a Mum and Dad
"And I just want to be free!"

"So if we find a kindly king
"Who will let a pirate in
"I bet that he will be a king
"Who can help you find some kin!"

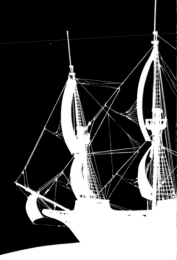

So their voyage had begun
With the wind against their backs
Their sails were full of salty sea air
And their bags all nice and packed.

Now of all the places the Cap'n had been
There was one for sure he didn't want in.
"I'm not going home. I'll never go back!
"Those people are mean and their king is a quack!"

"I left that place forever behind
"Pigs will fly before I change my mind!
"So if you tell me that I should live there
"You'd have better luck if you tried grabbing the air!"

8

The first country they put in
Was the island of GaZan
"Squids, let's go ask about their king
"Is he a nice old man?"

GaZan looked wonderful!
Every house was just so!
The barns and fields and
stores were full
"They must have lots of dough!"

But one thing they noticed
That just wasn't quite right
No one was smiling!
Their frowns were stuck tight!

"Excuse me, sir," said Flop, to
a man as they passed by
"No one here seems happy.
Can you tell us why?"

"Get lost, kid! I don't have time!
"I've way too much to do!
"Our mean old king will have my hide
"If I'm late because of you!"

"Cap'n Patch," said Flip,
"I could be wrong
"But I don't think this place will do!
"I do not think a crabby king
"Would like a guy like you!"

Off they sailed to another place
The sails were full and strong
"Let's dock and see if our
search is done," said Flop
"I hope it won't be long!"

"Welcome to AyMaw,"
the mayor declared.
"What can we do for you?"
"We'd like to learn about
your king," said Patch
"And your people too!"

"Our king is mighty, our king is fierce
"Our jails are full of crooks!
"We don't like folks who
raise their hand
"Or read unkingly books!
"And if we ever asked a question
"Our king would want our head!
"So we are very, very, very quiet
"And careful where we tread."

Flip was shocked!
"I don't think this joint is
where we should live!
"This king is mean! He doesn't forgive!"

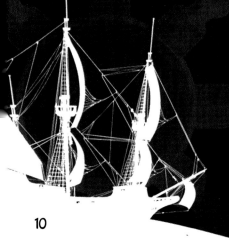

QUIET

11

"I know that we will find a place,"
Said Flop to Cap'n Patch.
"Where pirates and orphans
can feel at home
"And itches all get a good scratch!"

"Suppose'n a pirate had changed
his ways," pondered Patch
"And decided it's time to be good!
"Could he live here? Could
you believe him?
"There must be SOME
king that would!"

"I know you!" the Mayor said.
"You're that old rat fink Patch!
"Our king's been looking for you!
"You sank all his ships!
You stole all his toys!
"And ate all his ice cream, too!"

"I guess the only thing
to do," said Patch
"Is find a Happy Place
"Where you two squids
can find a home
"And no one knows my face!"

It was dark and dank when
they found KneeFall
They docked and went into town.
Every house was locked up tight
Not a pop or a peep was found!

Most of the homes were normal sized
But some were super gimongous!
Then suddenly, from the
shadows a man called out!
"Ho! There be strangers among us!"

"Hello, kind sir," said Flip to the man
"We're looking for a place to live.
"Is your king kindly? Can
pirates change for good?
"Does your king forgive?"

The man asked them all to "Shhhhhh!"
He was very afraid!
"Lo, if there but were such a king!
"T'would be a match in heaven made!

"Our land is ruled by giant men
"Though men they may not be
"They are ugly and smelly
and boss us all around
"And not only that, they're mean!"

"We'll help you find a home," said Flip
"There must be some king near
"Who forgives the rotten
and the sorry
"We'll find him! Do not fear!"

And so the ship sailed far away
Until it came to shore
"This place looks good! Let's
take a peek!" said Patch
"Let's try this one time more!"

"Our king?!" laughed the
Mayor. "That old bum?
"We fired him yesterday!
"We hated his rules and laws and now
"There's no one to make us obey!"

Back at sea, Cap'n Patch
had had enough!
His hopes were almost sank
"Now look here, compass!
"You find us a Good King
"Or I'll make you walk the plank!"

They went from country to country
And talked to king after king
And this is what all of them said:
"If we ever, ever, EVER catch
that old Pirate Patch
"We'll hang him until he is DEAD!"

Everywhere they went, the
story was the same:
"Pirates will NOT be forgiven!
"We'll throw them in jail!
"We'll make them eat mud!
"Their life will not be worth livin'!"

Ol' Patch kept his word: he
tossed out the compass!
"You blankety blank piece of junk!"
Right away, Patch knew he goofed twice
His temper had got him sunk!

Without a compass our heroes were lost
They did not know where to steer!
The ship went willy nilly and to and fro
From there and back to here!

Have you ever been lost? It's not very fun!
Not only were they lost, they were stuck!
The entire sea had turned to seaweed!
"Well, squids," said Patch, "that's my luck!"

The breeze was gone! The
seaweeds were like glue!
For days the ship held fast
Not only that, but their
candy bars were gone!
How long would their hope last?

Flip and Flop began to cry
"We'll never find a home!
"We're gonna croak in this seaweed sea
"We'll always be alone!"

"Cheer up, my squids! We'll get through this!
"I've been in tougher spots!"
"Like when?" asked Flop
"Well, back in Kooka Munga," Patch
said, "the savage cannibals
"Had me all tied up in knots!"

"How'd ya get out, Cap'n?"
Flip was amazed

"Good goofus!" said Flop.
"What'd ya do?"

"Well, my squids, yer ol'
Cap'n was at the end!

"I was gonna be Cap'n Patch stew!"

"It's the strangest thing! I
can't explain it," Patch said

"But suddenly they all ran away!

"Then this Royal Feller shows
up from nowhere and says

"'Patch, today's your day!'"

"And then, a dove landed
on my shoulder!

"He whispered, 'Patch, ya
aughtta be good!

"'Being naughty is not
working out!' he said

"'Why don't you try living
life as you should?'"

"So I don't know how

"And I don't know when

"But I know beyond a doubt

"Somewhere someone's
watching out for us

"And somehow we'll all get out!"

The very next morning the clouds began to churn
They turned as black as night
And then it hit! A monster typhoon!
"Hang on, my squids! We're going for a ride!"

All day and all night the ship was smashed
By storm and wind and sea
But when morning finally came, the wind and weed were gone!
The typhoon had set them free!

"I thought that we were goners," said Flip
"And that the typhoon would be the end!"
"It saved our lives!" said Flop. "It surely did!"
"That storm was really a friend!"

That evening every sail fell limp
The grey air chilled their bones
"Hang me temper!" said Patch. "We're blind and lost!
"I sent our compass to Davy Jones!"

"Confound this fog!" said Flip. "How can we find land?
"This fog's too thick to see it!"
"Hey, look, you two!" said Flop.
"This fog is so thick
"We could grab a chunk and eat it!"

And then the next morn, through pea soup fog
"I hear breakers!" yelled Flip.
"At last! Good ears, my squid!" said Patch
"The end of our long trip!"

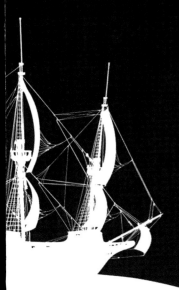

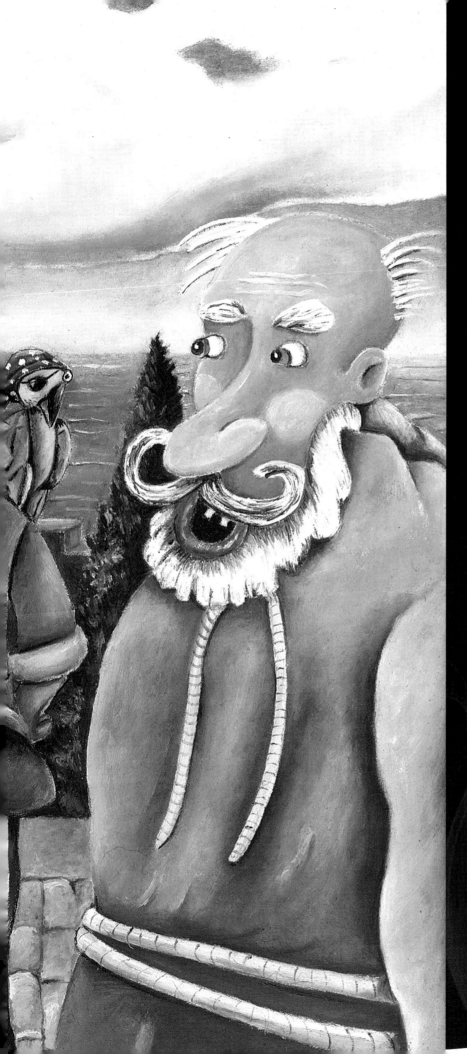

They docked the ship with jaws agape
And saw to their surprise
"The streets!" said Flop.
"They're made of gold!
"I can't believe my eyes!"

"Hey, you!" yelled Patch to a
distinguished passerby
"What kind of town is this?
"You pave your streets
with bricks of gold?
"It's not a sight to miss!"

"Our village is swell," the
gentleman replied
"The King demands it so.
"But if you like this,
check out HIS town!
"Now THAT'S the place to go!"

Patch and Flip and Flop
could not believe it!
"You have a king that's nice?"
"There's no one our King hasn't
seen and loved," the man said
"Be it people, bugs, or mice!"

Our heroes' eyes grew
as big as a house!
Could this place be really true?
"Cap'n," said Flop, "if this king
could love even snakes and bats
"He could love a skunk like you!"

25

"Would you like to see the King's
Town?" the kind gent offered
"I can take you there! They
call me the Proph
"And my favorite way to travel
"Is to travel by the air!"

The country looked peaceful
The farms were all clean
People smiled and waved
as they flew by
Not one soul was mean!

"I think we finally found
a place," said Patch
"For pirates bad like me!
"If this King is who I think He is
"We might just be home free!"

The King's town was awesome!
It was all new and bright
Everyone was friendly
Even the garbage smelled nice!

"I understand you'd like to live
"In the King's home land!
"Follow me!" said the Proph.
"I love our King!
"Our King is simply grand!"

But there were some in the
land who hated the King!
NoGosh was their leader
And pride was his thing!

28

"Good morning, Prophessor!" he grinned an evil grin
"I'll gladly take over now
"You know how I love to brag on my land
"And show new folks around!"

"Well, well, well! What have we here!
"Two mutts and one big snake!
"Sure, you can live here!
"There's just one catch...
"YOU GOTTA PAY FOR ALL YOUR MISTAKES!"

"Say," said Flop, "haven't we seen him somewhere before?"
"One thing's for sure," replied Flip
"He's crummy right down to the core!"

"My dear, Patch!" NoGosh was shocked.
"You've ran up quite a bill!
"Of all the rotten rats and thieves
"You are the king of the highest hill!

"If you think you can pay off this debt
"You're absolutely crackers
"Because I've been keeping count
"And it all adds up to forty nine hundred thousand
"BAZILLION GADZILLION SMACKERS!"

"What about my squids?" asked Patch.
"They never did no wrong!"

"They're hanging out with you, aren't they?
"They won't be good for long!"

NoGosh hauled our friends
off to the jailer

And Patch said, "Hey! I remember him!

"He's the meanest buzzard
I ever sailed with!

"Yer a dirty traitor, Squim!"

"If it's not me ol' shipmate
Patch!" said Squim

"You're gonna hate it in here!

"Not only does it smell; there's
no singin', no women, and—

"Aw, Squim, don't tell me—"

"Yup!" grinned Squim. "NO BEER!"

The jail was full of evil, mean villains
As far as the eye could see
But one guy stood out
He was beat up pretty bad
But he looked like Royalty!

"Howdy, Patch!" the Royal Feller
said. "How've ya been?
"I guess today's not your day!"
"For a minute," said Patch, "I
thought I'd finally found a king
"Whose rules would let me stay!"

"Some say we have many
rules here, Patch
"In fact, we have but two:
"'Love the King and serve Him well!'"
"That is our greatest rule
"The second one, though,
is even harder:
"'Be your neighbor's friend!'"
"By the time you crack that nut
"Your time down here will end!"

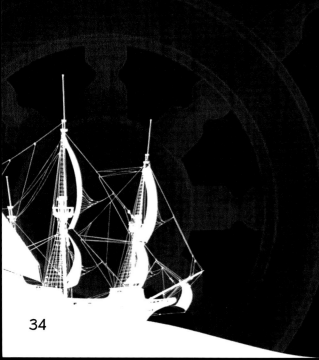

"What the heck are you in
here for?" asked Patch

"I thought your king is good!"

"My King is tops," the Royal Feller said

"But some didn't think I led my sheep

"The way a good shepherd should!"

"I've kissed a lot of pretty gals," said Patch

"And stolen many pies.

"You would not believe the naughty things

"I've seen with my own eyes!

"But now I'd like to change my ways

"And leave my past behind

"I want to be a man of peace

"And only do what's kind!"

"I've heard it said our people are
mean," the Royal Feller sighed

"And our King is just a quack!

"Well, some squids are blind,
but some refuse to see

"It's wisdom that they lack.

"So you've searched the whole
wide world for a king!

"Tell me, Patch, what did you find?

"The world is so big, and kings are so many

"There must be hundreds that are kind!"

"I've seen some kings get voted in," replied Patch
"Some are kings from birth
"Some kings fight and steal to get their thrones
"They all lie about their worth!"

"I found kings that were unruly mobs
"And some were ugly giants
"I found that all of them will shut you up
"If you are not compliant!"

"Some kings would have me rot in jail
"Some would have me hang
"But I never found a single king
"Who was worth a DING DONG DANG!"

"Tell us about this king of
yours!" begged Flop

"What kind of guy is he?"

"Would he care that Cap'n Patch is
not the buzzard he used to be?"

"I guess you could say I know
our King pretty well

"So I'll tell you what He would say:

"'I go absolutely bonkers
when rotten pirates

"'Knock it off and change their ways!'

"He'd say, 'I don't care about your
past or what you used to be

"'If you're really sorry and turn about

"'You get a brand new start with me!'"

The Royal Feller stayed
up late that night

Explaining Kingly tales

While Flip and Flop and Patch
all dreamed the same dream

Of a ship that had no sails!

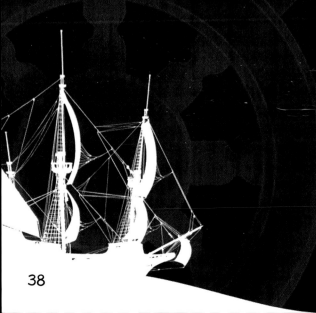

Suddenly, during the black of night
They awoke to a knock on the wall!
It was Squim, Cap'n
Patch's old shipmate!
He did not look happy at all!

"OK, shepherd, the weekend's over!
"We gotta letcha go!
"But we don't like you or
your brand-new pals
"So make like the trade
winds and blow!"

"My time is up," the Royal Feller
said. "It's been three days
"It's been nice meeting you!
"If I see the King, and I'm sure I will
"I'll see what He can do!"

"As for you three," said Squim,
"your bill is not paid!
"Yer stuck in this stinkhole forever!
"My boss says you are his
favorite prisoners
"And the day you'll get out is NEVER!"

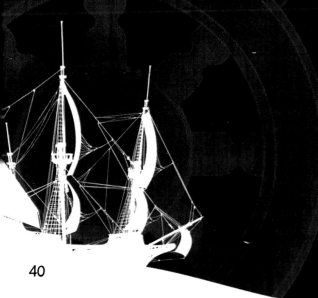

"I'm sorry, my squids!" Patch said with despair. "I let you down!
"We're gonna rot here because of me!
"Don't say that, Cap'n!" Flip replied. "Remember Kooka Munga?
"Somebody helped you get free!"

"Yeah!" agreed Flop. "What about the seaweed?
"And the fog! The typhoon, the lost compass?
"We're not givin' up, and you'd better not neither!
"This jail ain't gonna whump us!"

"For all the crummy things I've done," said Patch
"This is what I deserve
"But my poor squids! Your only crime
"Was choosing me to serve!"

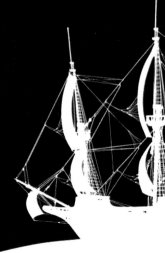

"Now, Cap'n!" said Flip. "You've been our friend!
"We're not ditching you now!
"You're not a rat anymore," added Flop
"And besides, we love you!"
"You love me?"
They both replied, "AND HOW!"

The two gave Cap'n Patch a great big hug
And kissed him on the cheek
And even with all the stink and snoring
They had a wonderful, peaceful sleep!

Then early in the morning
Before the sun or roosters rose
Squim was back! So was
the Proph! He said
"This place hurts my nose!"

"It seems that someone paid
your bill!" growled Squim
"We've gotta letcha go!
"But who'd be dumb enough
to do such a thing?
"I'd really like to know!"

"You know very well who paid
their bill!" said the Proph
"He's the very one you hate!
"How many times do I have to say it?
"The one you hate is great!"

"My King is throwing a big
party in your honor, Cap'n
"And there are two things
He told me to say:
"'I'm absolutely bonkers
about you, Patch!' and
"'Welcome home! Today's your day!'"

"If you would like," said the Proph

"Our King has a ship

"It's the fastest in the fleet!

"But she needs a Captain

"And two very special mates

"To make her crew complete!"

"Could we, Cap'n?" Flip
bounced with hope

"Could we sail with you?'

"We'll be good mates!" Flop
begged on bended knee

"Could we be part of your crew?"

"Well, my squids," the Cap'n
rubbed his whiskers

"You ARE my mates!

"And if this King of ours is true

"We'll be mates forever!

"And as He has loved us

"I'm absolutely bonkers about you!"

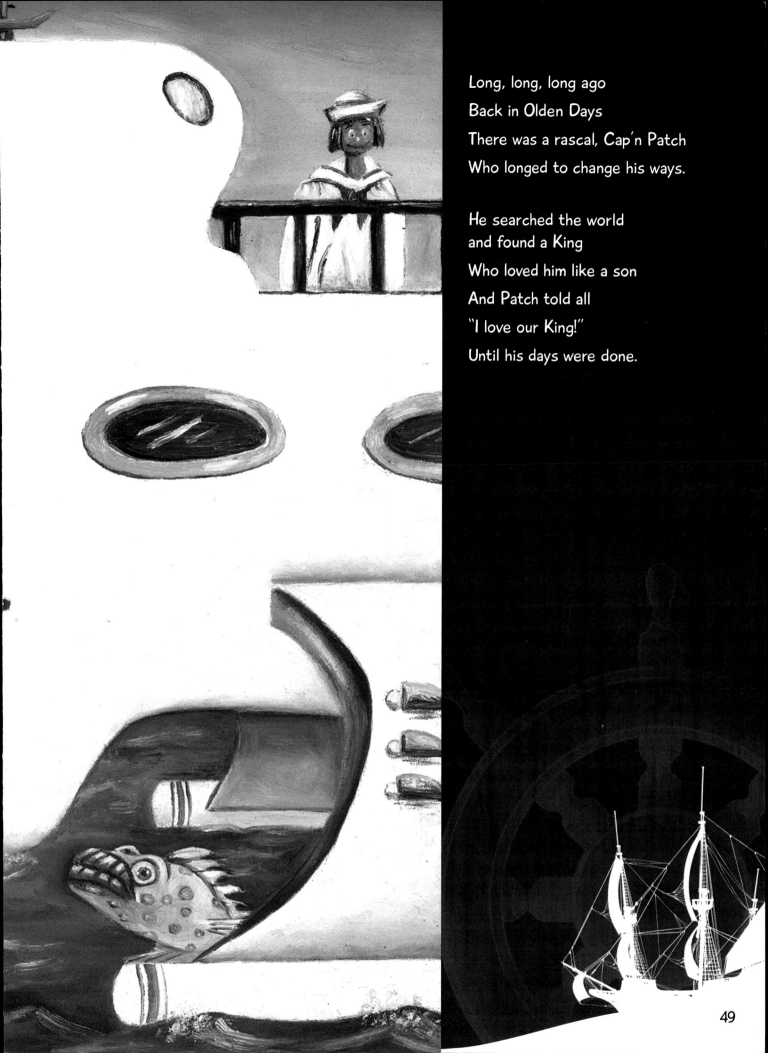

Long, long, long ago
Back in Olden Days
There was a rascal, Cap'n Patch
Who longed to change his ways.

He searched the world
and found a King
Who loved him like a son
And Patch told all
"I love our King!"
Until his days were done.

"What, you say? He bailed them out? He paid for every crime?

"Foiled again! I hate that guy! He does that all the time!"

To King searchers everywhere
I dedicate this book
He's out there, all right:
If you've the guts to look!

A Jewish rabbi once asked, "Why do you call me 'good'?" As a student of world history and cultures, Ronald Wayne Fry has long been fascinated with mankind's hunger for a strong global leader.

Growing up as a Midwest farm boy who later ventured all over North America and China, Ron's first book explores a search for that one good king.

Ron and his wife Christy reside in the beautiful rolling farmlands of northwestern Illinois, and serve in their church's Kidz ministry. In addition to his family, Ron is nuts about Jesus, airplanes, and the Green Bay Packers.

Terry Werntz retired from teaching art in 2011. He received his college education at Northern Illinois University. He now makes his home in northwestern Illinois and lives with his wife Janet and their two cats Wafer and Lover Dover. His first book "Grace the Church Mouse", which he authored and illustrated was published in 2011. "The Good King" has allowed him to bring another author's words to life through his oil painted illustrations. His youngest grandson, Domminick posed for the characters of Flip and Flop.